KU-271-981

ALL ABOUT ME TOO

Name	Nelly
Age	Five-ish
Getting up time	mornings (mainly)
Bedtime	as late as possible
Max speed (walking) (running)	My mummy says I never walk anywear 50,000,000,000½ mph
School	Not if I can help it
Likes	football, woodwork, welding, mending things, fast food, Slimey the snail
Dislikes	school, people wot SAY they don't like children's TV when they do, having my hair combed, carrots.
Running away fund	50p
Best moment	Sticking Lil's hat down the ~~bog toilet~~ lavatory
Ambitions	to be a strong man, or a pop star, or a van driver

For Rosie and Beth
JW

This edition published in Picture Lions by HarperCollins Publishers Ltd in 1999
First published in hardback by HarperCollins Publishers Ltd in 1998

3 5 7 9 10 8 6 4 2

ISBN: 0 00 664 653-0

Picture Lions is an imprint of the Children's Division,
part of HarperCollins Publishers Ltd, 77-85 Fulham Palace Road, Hammersmith, London W6 8JB.
Text and illustrations copyright © John Wallace 1998
The author/illustrator asserts the moral right to be identified as the author/illustrator of the work.
A CIP catalogue record for this title is available from the British Library.
All rights reserved. No part of this publication may be reproduced, stored in a retrieval system
or transmitted in any form or by any means, electronic, mechanical, photocopying, recording
or otherwise, without the prior permission of HarperCollins Publishers Ltd,
77-85 Fulham Palace Road, Hammersmith, London W6 8JB.
The HarperCollins website address is: www.fireandwater.com
Printed and bound in Singapore by Imago

The Twins

FALKIRK COUNCIL
LIBRARY SUPPORT
FOR SCHOOLS

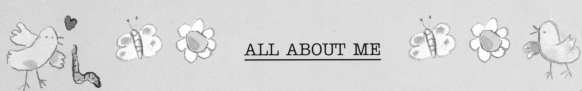

ALL ABOUT ME

Name	Lil
Age	four years, eleven months and five days
Getting up time	06.15 hours
Bedtime	Mon – Fri: 8.25 pm Saturday: watch 9 o'clock news
Maximum Speed (walking) (running)	1 mile per hour ~~I never run~~ much slower than my sister
~~Education~~ School	Primary school
Likes	pink, school programmes, hoovering and dusting, wearing sensible shoes, carrots and other healthy foods, neat and tidy things
Dislikes	silly people, children's television, rough games like playing pirates, burgers and other fatty foods, my computer breaking down
~~Savings~~ cash	I have £21.45 in my 'Pennymistress Account'
Best moment	Learning how to work my computer
Ambitions	To become a teacher, an air hostess, or a princess

The Twins

John Wallace

PictureLions
An Imprint of HarperCollinsPublishers

Lil and Nelly were coming home from
school. Their class had been set a project
and there was a prize for the best one.
"I'm going to write all about me," said Lil.
"Well, I'm going to play," said Nelly.

"Tap, tap, tap, tappety-tap!" Lil started
to type out her project.

She worked so hard
that she had finished
by teatime.

Nelly decided to have
a look at what Lil had written.
"There's not enough about me in it," she thought.

Nelly sat down and started to add
to her sister's project.

ALL ABOUT ME
BY LIL

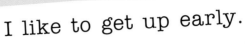

I like to get up early.

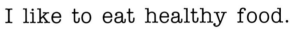

I like to eat healthy food.

I like the school
programmes.

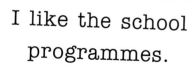

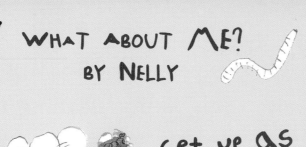

WHAT ABOUT ME?
BY NELLY

Get up as late
as possible

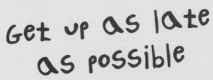

cake for breakfast

I like the lions wots on TV

My favourite thing is my cleaning kit.

My pet rabbit

is called Fluffy.

My hair is smooth

and blonde.

I love my spade

My pet is
Slimey
the Snail

My mum
says my hair
looks like a
haystack

THINGS I LIKE

school

pink

classical music

dressing up

hoovering

and dusting

THINGS I DON'T LIKE

people who eat with their fingers

smells

dirt

fatty foods
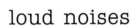

loud noises

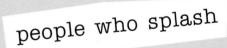

people who splash

and make a mess

When I grow up...

I want to be a teacher

or an air hostess

or a princess.

Nelly was just putting
the project back
where she had found it,
when Lil walked in.
"Nelly, what are you
doing?" asked Lil.

"Oh!" said Nelly.
"I was just reading
your project.
Isn't it great!"

"Have you done yours yet?" asked Lil, later.
"Oh, yes," said Nelly, with a smile.

That night, Lil dreamed she had won
the prize for the best project.

Nelly dreamed that Slimey the Snail
had eaten Lil's project for breakfast.

The next morning, Lil saw
what Nelly had done.

She didn't speak to Nelly
all the way to school.

The class sat quietly,
while the teacher marked the projects.

Finally, the teacher said, "The prize for the best project goes to Lil *and* Nelly."

The twins couldn't believe it.

"By the way, whose idea was it to do
the project together?" asked the teacher.

"Both of us had the idea *together*,"
said Nelly triumphantly.
"Oh, yes," Lil had to agree. "We always
do everything together!"

ALL ABOUT ME

Name	Lil
Age	four years, eleven months and five days
Getting up time	06.15 hours
Bedtime	Mon – Fri: 8.25 pm Saturday: watch 9 o'clock news
Maximum Speed (walking) (running)	1 mile per hour ~~I never run~~ *much slower than my sister*
~~Education~~ School	Primary school
Likes	pink, school programmes, hoovering and dusting, wearing sensible shoes, carrots and other healthy foods, neat and tidy things
Dislikes	silly people, children's television, rough games like playing pirates, burgers and other fatty foods, my computer breaking down
~~Savings~~ cash	I have £21.45 in my 'Pennymistress Account'
Best moment	Learning how to work my computer
Ambitions	To become a teacher, an air hostess, or a princess

ALL ABOUT ME TOO

Name	Nelly
Age	Five-ish
Getting up time	mornings (mainly)
Bedtime	as late as possible
Max speed (walking) (running)	My mummy says I never walk anywear 50,000,000,000½ mph
School	Not if I can help it
Likes	football, woodwork, welding, mending things, fast food, Slimey the snail
Dislikes	School, people wot SAY they don't like children's TV when they do, having my hair combed, carrots.
Running away fund	50p
Best moment	Sticking Lil's hat down the ~~bog toilet~~ lavatory
Ambitions	to be a strong man, or a pop star, or a van driver

FALKIRK COUNCIL
LIBRARY SUPPORT
FOR SCHOOLS